A Note to Parents and Caregivers:

Read-it! Readers are for children who are just starting on the amazing road to reading. These beautiful books support both the acquisition of reading skills and the love of books.

 The PURPLE LEVEL presents basic topics and objects using high frequency words and simple language patterns.

 The RED LEVEL presents familiar topics using common words and repeating sentence patterns.

 The BLUE LEVEL presents new ideas using a larger vocabulary and varied sentence structure.

 The YELLOW LEVEL presents more challenging ideas, a broad vocabulary, and wide variety in sentence structure.

 The GREEN LEVEL presents more complex ideas, an extended vocabulary range, and expanded language structures.

 The ORANGE LEVEL presents a wide range of ideas and concepts using challenging vocabulary and complex language structures.

When sharing a book with your child, read in short stretches, pausing often to talk about the pictures. Have your child turn the pages and point to the pictures and familiar words. And be sure to reread favorite stories or parts of stories.

There is no right or wrong way to share books with children. Find time to read with your child, and pass on the legacy of literacy.

Adria F. Klein, Ph.D.
Professor Emeritus
California State University
San Bernardino, California

Editor: Jill Kalz
Designer: Nathan Gassman
Page Production: Ellen Schofield
Associate Managing Editor: Christianne Jones
The illustrations in this book were created with watercolor.

Picture Window Books
5115 Excelsior Boulevard
Suite 232
Minneapolis, MN 55416
877-845-8392
www.picturewindowbooks.com

Printed in the United States of America.

Library of Congress Cataloging-in-Publication Data
Williams, Jacklyn.
Let's go fishing, Gus! / by Jacklyn Williams ; illustrated by Doug Cushman.
p. cm. — (Read-it! readers. Gus the hedgehog)
Summary: Gus knows nothing about fishing, but his grandfather teaches him all
of the important things—including that there is more to a great fishing trip than
catching fish.
ISBN-13: 978-1-4048-2713-4 (hardcover)
ISBN-10: 1-4048-2713-7 (hardcover)
[1. Fishing—Fiction. 2. Grandfathers—Fiction. 3. Hedgehogs—Fiction.]
I. Cushman, Doug, ill. II. Title. III. Title: Let us go fishing, Gus! IV. Series.
PZ7.W6656Let 2006
[E]—dc22
                                                    2006003381

Read-it! Readers
Orange Level

Let's Go Fishing, Gus!

by Jacklyn Williams
illustrated by Doug Cushman

Special thanks to our advisers for their expertise:

Adria F. Klein, Ph.D.
Professor Emeritus, California State University
San Bernardino, California

Susan Kesselring, M.A.
Literacy Educator
Rosemount–Apple Valley–Eagan (Minnesota) School District

PICTURE WINDOW BOOKS
Minneapolis, Minnesota

The doorbell rang, and Gus ran to answer it.

"Are you ready to go fishing?" Grandpa asked.

"You bet!" said Gus.

4

Gus' mom gave both of them a hug goodbye
and told Gus to be good.

"I will," Gus said. "Get the frying pan ready,"
he added. "Grandpa and I are going to catch
a million fish today!"

Once they got to the lake, Gus and Grandpa slid the canoe off the truck and carried it down to the water.

"Before we go, we need to check our tackle," said Grandpa.

"What's tackle?" asked Gus.

"Things such as fishing poles, fishing line, hooks, and bait are tackle," said Grandpa.

Gus looked worried.

"Did you pack your fishing pole, fishing line, hook, and bait, Gus?" asked Grandpa.

Gus shook his head.

"Well, what did you bring?" asked Grandpa.

"I brought lots of other good stuff," said Gus.

Gus picked up his backpack and shook it.
Out fell a stick of chewing gum, a piece of
string, a can of spaghetti, and a safety pin.

"Hmmm," Grandpa said. "Let's see. What can we do with all of this?"

He picked up the stick of gum and handed it to Gus. "Chew this," he said.

While Gus chewed, Grandpa found a branch.
He tied the string to one end. Then he tied the
safety pin to the end of the string.

Next, Grandpa opened the can of spaghetti.
He pulled out a slippery noodle and wrapped
it around the safety pin.

Grandpa held out his hand. "Gum, please," he said.

"Why do you want my gum?" asked Gus.

"You'll see," said Grandpa. Then he stuck the gum on the noodle to hold it in place.

"You were right," Grandpa continued, looking at the new fishing pole. "You did bring lots of other good stuff."

Grandpa and Gus climbed into the canoe and shoved off. At first, the canoe turned in circles.

"We have to row together, in the same direction," said Grandpa, "or we'll get dizzy!"

16

Grandpa and Gus tried again. This time the
canoe moved in a straight line, right to the
middle of the lake.

"This looks like a good spot for fish," said
  Grandpa, dropping his line into the water.

"When will the fish start biting?" Gus asked.

"Soon," said Grandpa.

18

After a couple minutes, Gus sighed. "Why aren't the fish biting yet?" he asked.

"They will," said Grandpa. "We just need to wait."

"Maybe they don't know we're waiting," said Gus.

"You're right," Grandpa said. "Maybe they
need a song to bring them along."

Grandpa started to sing, and Gus joined in:

Catfish, o catfish,
please come here to me.
You'd make a fine supper,
swimming 'round my tummy.

After awhile, Grandpa and Gus stopped
singing. They waited ... and waited ... and
waited. Neither of them got a nibble.

21

Soon, the sun started to set. It was time to go home.

Gus started to pull in his line, but something on the other end pulled back.

"You've got a fish, Gus!" yelled Grandpa.

Gus pulled and pulled.

"It's the biggest fish ever!" yelled Grandpa.
"Keep pulling!"

Gus pulled on his line as hard as he could.

"You've got it!" exclaimed Grandpa. "You've got a big ... black ... BOOT!"

Gus stood up for a closer look.

"Don't stand up in the—" Grandpa yelled.

But it was too late. The canoe tipped, and—
SPLOOSH! SPLASH!—Gus and Grandpa
tumbled into the lake.

As the canoe bobbed upside down, the soggy
fishermen swam back to shore.

"Oh, look at the canoe," said Gus sadly.

"Don't worry," said Grandpa. "I'll get it."

Grandpa cast out his fishing line. ZING! The line flew across the water. TWANG! The hook snagged the canoe, and Grandpa pulled the line tight.

"Great catch!" said Gus.

Grandpa and Gus dragged the canoe out of the lake, loaded it onto the truck, and headed for home.

"Sorry we didn't catch any fish, Gus," said Grandpa. "But we had a good time, didn't we?"

"We sure did!" said Gus.

Grandpa honked the horn as he and Gus
pulled into the driveway. Gus' mom came out
to meet them.

"How was your fishing trip?" she asked.

"It was great!" Gus said. Then he sniffled and snuffled. "We made a fishing pole. We sang to the fish. I caught a boot, and Grandpa caught the canoe. ACHOO! ACHOO!"

"And it sounds like you caught a cold, too,"
Mom said. "But did you two catch any fish?"

"No," said Gus. "But it doesn't matter. It was
the best fishing trip ever!"

More *Read-it!* Readers

Bright pictures and fun stories help you practice your reading skills. Look for more books at your level.

Happy Birthday, Gus! 1-4048-0957-0

Happy Easter, Gus! 1-4048-0959-7

Happy Halloween, Gus! 1-4048-0960-0

Happy Thanksgiving, Gus! 1-4048-0961-9

Happy Valentine's Day, Gus! 1-4048-0962-7

Matt Goes to Mars 1-4048-1269-5

Merry Christmas, Gus! 1-4048-0958-9

Rumble Meets Buddy Beaver 1-4048-1287-3

Rumble Meets Chester the Chef 1-4048-1335-7

Rumble Meets Eli Elephant 1-4048-1332-2

Rumble Meets Keesha Kangaroo 1-4048-1290-3

Rumble Meets Milly the Maid 1-4048-1341-1

Rumble Meets Penny Panther 1-4048-1331-4

Rumble Meets Sylvia and Sally Swan 1-4048-1541-4

Rumble Meets Wally Warthog 1-4048-1289-X

Welcome to Third Grade, Gus! 1-4048-2714-5

Looking for a specific title or level? A complete list of *Read-it!* Readers is available on our Web site: **www.picturewindowbooks.com**